WHO HAUNTS THIS HOUSE?

ISBN: 979-8-9866137-0-3 (paperback)

ISBN: 979-8-9866137-1-0 (Kindle)

"If you are looking for a book that is family friendly with a deeper, serious meaning, *Who Haunts This House* is for you. The book is a treatment of the legend of the ghost of the Yellow House in Tiverton, RI, with a backward glance to Washington Irving's *Legend of Sleepy Hollow*. On a deeper level, it describes the main character's search to find himself and then act on his newfound self-knowledge. His journey is not all that uncommon as we struggle to find our role in the world of the pandemic. It is a great book for the family especially if you are looking for a good Halloween read."

Charles Beiter, Professor of English, Waynesburg University

* * *

"To curate wax figures that appear authentic can be a *haunting* task especially when you discover *shocking* surprises in this Halloween story."

Willie Wideman-Pleasants, Co-chair for the National Writers Union/Boston Chapter, and author of several books, including **Make Truth a Habit**

It is Tiverton, Rhode Island, in the specific neighborhood known as Four Corners, surrounded by the history and folklore of old New England. The year is 1820.

Or is it, really? Let's correct the record; the year is 2020.

Or is it, really? Perhaps it's both?

The story of *Who Haunts This House* began with the imagination of the founder and director of the Neighborhood Players of Four Corners, in Tiverton, Rhode Island. After growing up across the street from the historic Soule-Seabury *Yellow House*, Bobby Sylvia wanted to share a stage play about a local history as the setting for a story about a universal history, finding ourselves in the midst of a pandemic much like the smallpox pandemic of 200 years ago.

That stage script by author Jed Griswold then became this novella, sharing the backstory of the events, rooted in local history, and the characters, rooted in our imagination.

ACKNOWLEDGMENTS

Many thanks to Bobby Sylvia, the founder of the *Neighborhood Players* of Four Corners, in Tiverton, RI, who offered me the opportunity to develop his original concept of a museum filled with wax figures and ghosts into a stage script. That script led to this novella, adding a historical and fictional backstory and adding a character. Bobby created a story in skeleton form, awaiting the script and novella to add sinew and flesh to the bones. Without the skeleton, and Bobby's support, this embellishment would not have matured.

Note that the Soule-Seabury family is a factual part of Tiverton history, but the museum and the names of the children and the main modern-day characters and events are fictional. But we will let *you* decide whether the ghost(s) are factual or fictional...

Many thanks also to Charles Beiter and Janet Naaktgeboren for being very helpful critical readers and volunteer editors.

ALSO BY THIS AUTHOR

The Power of Storytelling, Wood Lake Publishing, and available on Amazon
A Great Retirement, Griswold Consulting, info@griswoldconsulting.net

TABLE of CONTENTS

PART 1: THE PAST

PART 2: THE PRESENT

JED GRISWOLD

Griswold
Consulting

info @ griswoldconsulting.net

WHO HAUNTS THIS HOUSE?

A novella based on an original concept by
Bobby Sylvia

Cover drawing of the Soule-Seabury House by
Christopher P. Griswold

PART 1: THE PAST

Chapter 1 – How it all began

It was not a dark and stormy night. In fact, it was a crisp autumn evening when sunset was late enough to keep the stars at bay. It all started in plain sight, though Tim couldn't see it.

Timothy Allen Wilson, known as Tim by his twin sister and friends, had recently returned home to the neighborhood known as "Four Corners" in Tiverton, RI. Though Tim's birth certificate name was indeed "Timothy," he was never comfortable with the full name; it seemed to him too formal and when he used it the result was a more distant interaction with others. An outgoing and friendly extravert, he always preferred informal connections with people and he used that style to complement his unassuming personality.

Tim's twin sister, Theresa Leah Wilson, was named after her great Aunt. She was often told that she resembled her in appearance and personality though she had never known her, as her aunt died shortly after Theresa was born. "Theresa" quickly became "Terry," though she gradually preferred the full and more proper form as she matured and started her own business. It was a better fit, as she was the more formal and reserved introvert of the two.

Tim and Terry were the descendants of many generations of Tiverton, Rhode Island families who throughout that long history, closely interacted socially, economically and culturally. The local environment encouraged that, and as a result, everyone knew their neighbors if not the entire village's inhabitants. It was, indeed, *home*, a place where one could feel grounded and safe.

Among their group of closest friends, most became successful after high school graduation. Robert opened a photography business after winning several regional competitions shortly after graduation; Suzie, who had been the Homecoming Queen her senior year, expanded her mother's dress shop; Pat, who had been the go-to offensive linebacker during Tim's quarterbacking years, became the town's police chief, continuing his mission of "protecting and defending" the team, and he eventually married Terry; Abby started an art supply store; Ann, the editor of the high school newspaper, became a reporter for a local paper; and Carol, who belonged to the school radio club, became a reporter for a local radio station. They were a tight-knit support group for each other, an important aspect of gaining confidence in one's ability to succeed in every aspect of life.

Tim was the only one of the close "townie" group to leave Tiverton soon after graduation with high hopes of continuing his winning days, after being the star, record-setting quarterback all three years in high school. He majored in history in college and finished an MBA with a specialty in Museum Management. During graduate school, he completed two successful internships and one of them led to a position as the Assistant Curator of a major museum in Philadelphia.

He established his skills right away by demonstrating a creative touch to a new exhibit which required a family dressed in period costumes. The budget only allowed for the re-use of several mannequins which were in a long-ignored basement closet. Tim created and applied a special wax-based make-up of his own original recipe to use over the dummies' faces to make them look quite real. It was a technique he learned in a graduate seminar in art history. The general impact of the entire exhibit impressed his supervisor, and led to a promotion as *Assistant Director in Charge of Special Exhibits*. Five years later, when the position opened up, he was promoted to *Head Curator*. Though his friends sometimes worried about the challenges of being so far away from home, his venture into the big city had paid off. His dream of becoming known in the museum world was coming true.

Until...he was fired.

Chapter 2 – Tim returns home

It was a mystery, but some valuable items on prominent display in one of Tim's new exhibits, disappeared – simply *vanished* without a clue.

Among the missing pieces was a very valuable, signed, first edition book and several distinctive gold watches. It was clear to the police that these items were carefully targeted because they were small and easily smuggled out of the museum. And the timing was critical: the items were apparently removed at the end of the exhibit season, which meant that an inventory for the next season would not be taken for several months, leaving a cold and clueless trail.

There was no sign of a break-in. No broken windows or damaged locks. And the security cameras did not capture any unusual activity. Based on the evidence, or lack thereof, the investigation concluded that it must have been an "inside job." And given that lack of evidence, no one was charged with a crime, but *someone* had to be held accountable. And that responsibility, unfortunately, fell on Tim's shoulders...and

upon his conscience...and on his
resume...and in his memory.
After hoping for bigger and better things in
the bigger and brighter city, he found
himself in a smaller and darker lost place.

Which is why Tim moved back home,
explaining to Terry that "when you get lost,
home is a good place to be found."

That was one very endearing aspect of
Tim's personality: either creating a new
proverb, or rephrasing (to the point of
reinventing) an old and familiar one. But
never exactly repeating a known quote. The
proverb was always uniquely his, which
made it (and him) more memorable. And it
was always delivered with a grin. No one
remembered how or when it started. Perhaps
it was an intentional inspiration from his
creative side, or perhaps he couldn't recall
the actual saying, but however it began, it
became a "Tim Trademark." The trait made
his friends smile, and contributed to his
popularity.

One of his best known sayings was that
"history doesn't repeat, but it *does* rhyme."
The origin of the truism is unknown, but it
has been attributed to Mark Twain, Arnold
Tolstoy and Santayana, among others. But in

Tiverton, it was always attributed to Tim. He repeated it often as a history major, to argue that history could never really be duplicated because the effects of advances in technology, or cultural changes, or the social complexities of each new generation, all made history more complicated and with uniquely different aspects. These factors changed, but Tim did believe there were consistent themes in human living over the vast historical timeline, which kept reappearing around us – or perhaps *through* us.

Upon his firing, Tim thought now more and more about the positive period of his high school connections and successes, and those memories were now foremost in his mind; they were needed, especially now, to move aside the fearful memories of failure. Tim wondered if that *principle of rhyme* might apply to his personal history; returning home might find a repeated theme of success, anew, at home.

So, Tim returned home to find himself, or to be found again, or ... both...

Chapter 3 – The transition

But returning home at his age, empty handed
and empty-pocketed, was embarrassing. Not
only was he jobless but he was forced to
move in with Terry until he could get
established. It was not his expected image of
a homecoming for a winning quarterback.

At least his close relationship to his twin
was a source of stability, which Tim so
desperately needed now. Terry was a good
person be around in his isolated days.

In high school, Terry had not been an insider
among the most popular group of students.
She wasn't a wallflower by any means, but
she didn't have a 'following', in contrast to
her brother. Tim was probably the most
popular student in the school; he was the
classic football-star-hero, having led his
team for three years as the most winning
quarterback in the school's history, setting
several local and state records.

In contrast, as an introvert, Terry preferred
quiet, solo-style hobbies, instead of Tim's
large football celebrations. Compared to the
dozens of signatures in Tim's senior
yearbook, she had only a few as she had a
shorter list of friends, though, in true

introvert fashion, that shorter list included deeper friendships, while Tim's list included many more, mostly superficial connections. That happens sometimes with extroverted and more outgoing students.

Terry now owned her own business, working alone, as she preferred. It all started with a hobby kit, building a computer, and it evolved into a computer repair shop and then a full array of IT consulting services, including a specialty in setting up and maintaining security systems for local organizations, many established or continued by her classmates. Among them: Robert's photography store; Suzie's dress shop; a newly founded but not yet opened, non-profit museum, focusing on regional history; a locally owned bank; Abby's art store, now filled with a wide variety of creative works and art supplies; and Pat's police headquarters; and, through Ann and Carol, the local newspaper and radio stations.

A social network can offer more than an engine to foster emotional development; it also has the ability to empower a person's full business potential, as well. That certainly applied to Terry.

Her business began with these contacts with friends but soon thrived and grew as her personality traits were a good match for the IT business: she was a logical, sequential thinker, precise and punctual; she paid attention to details and stayed close to her estimated task-time-lines. In short, Terry had a "computer geek's mind." And she also had good entrepreneurial skills which helped her become the top "go-to" computer guru of Tiverton.

She was now more popular than Tim; their roles were ironically reversed: the introvert was receiving more attention than the extravert.

Sometimes role reversals can be lessons from our past and present...all building blocks for a better future...

Chapter 4 – A new door opens

Tim reluctantly accepted his sister's invitation to move into her home's spare bedroom. It had served as a storage space for computer parts, and Terry was able to make the necessary changes rather easily. Still, it was a small space, and relying on her felt uncomfortable. Nonetheless, he agreed, on the terms that he would move out as soon as he had found a job.

But the search for a job, even for the former star quarterback, proved to be as elusive as an NFL contract. Though he was welcomed back as a family welcomes home a lost puppy, not only was his resumé limited, it was tainted with a not-so-supportive reference from his previous employer. Tim's loss of hope began to tread close to a fear that he would be lost forever.

Until...Terry had an idea.

While installing a new security system for the fledgling museum at Four Corners, she learned that they were seeking a new special exhibit coordinator. It would be a full time job but on a limited contract depending on the museum's application for a new grant, and, more importantly, the success of the first season. Terry knew that a position with such a restrictive contract and a low compensation would be difficult to fill.

So she suggested Tim. And because of her well-established reputation the trustees agreed to make an offer.

Though she willingly took a risk for her twin brother, she did have a nagging fear that Tim would have a stumbling block: he was not a particularly well organized person. His office desk was always cluttered with papers laying at different angles and in no clearly defined stacks. Guessing which paper belonged in what file was a mystery to his co-workers, and it was sometimes an in-office game of predictions: "How long would it take for Tim to find a particular, early draft of an exhibit layout?" There was even an occasional penny-ante pool for the winner.

But somehow, whenever he was asked for a receipt or a design, he would intuitively remember where it was in the perceived chaos of his office. It was when he attempted a new filing system that he couldn't quickly find what he needed.

He was the type who would use a tool, like a screwdriver, and then place it on a nearby table or shelf, only to forget later, when he needed the tool again, where he last used it. He constantly had to retrace his steps to the spot where he may have previously set it aside.

Such efforts took more time than to have returned the tool in its proper storage place after using it, in a tool box or on a wall with other tools. But it simply wasn't in Tim's nature.

What *was* in his nature was the amazing ability to transform what is *seen with the five senses* into what *could be seen with a sixth sense*. That is the gift of a creative and vivid imagination. And that skill could never be stored away on a shelf or in a tool box, for it was ever on the move, in his mind and in his vision for the future – focusing on what *could be* but *is not yet.*

Terry, on the other hand, lived by the rule that required tools, or notes or pens, to live in a consistent home: a toolbox, a file, or a pencil holder. She was clearly as creative as Tim, but in a completely different way; she could problem-solve just about any computer related hiccup, but in her approach to finding creative solutions, as a reality-based person, it only made sense to be organized.

Which is why she worried about Tim.

Her fear was that he might create his own tripping points trying to organize a small, low-budget, new museum, staffed mostly by volunteers.

But Tim was so grateful - and a little desperate - that he quickly accepted the job offer. One immediate benefit was that he could move out of Terry's house, even if it meant sleeping on a cot in the basement of the museum. He also knew it was a step in a long range plan. His position as curator of the new museum in town, albeit with the restrictions, was an opportunity to raise the dimmer-switch of an overhead light on a dimming career, and to bring fresh air to the stifling living room of *real* life. In other words, it was an invitation to enter the door of hope.

So...Tim dived into his new role.

Chapter 5 – The museum curator: historian and researcher

The job of a museum curator is, to say it simply, like that of a multi-dimensional magician behind the curtains.

It all begins with research, sometimes through tangible sources such as newspaper articles, biographies, family records, court records, historical references, interviews and diaries. And sometimes the research also seeks out more *intangible* sources, such as the local folk lore.

It was in the folk lore that Tim learned more about something he vaguely remembered from his childhood in the neighborhood: *The Yellow House* (the location of the new museum) was haunted.

Some say the ghost was that of Abner Soule, who built the house around 1770. Others say it was the ghost of a revolutionary war soldier who disappeared in one of many skirmishes in an area of New England where tensions were high between physically close communities of British Loyalists or Colonialists. Perhaps it was a victim of the earlier *King Philip's War*, either an indigenous native or an invading settler.

Some even say that it was the ghost of a
Wampanoag Indian who lived in the land
that became Tiverton, Rhode Island, as their
own culture was increasingly threatened in
that era.

And still others say the ghost was that of
"Little George" Seabury, who lived and died
while "Big George" Washington was the
nation's first President.

Tim enthusiastically dived into the history –
and what would become the story – of the
new museum exhibit. He was particularly
intrigued by the questions around a ghost –
or *ghosts*. Was the explanation to be found
in a person or in the *personification* of a
hope...or of a fear?

These questions energized his imagination
and his creativity as Tim could identify with
a ghost born of either fear or hope, as he,
himself, was caught somewhere along the
continuum of these two poles of life.

Chapter 6 -- The museum curator: art designer

The next hat of the museum curator is that of an *artistic designer*.

How many displays would be needed to tell the story, and how would the exhibits be spaced, given the number of rooms and square footage available? How would the figures of the past be designed to be relatable to the modern-day museum visitor, drawing in their curiosity? How do rigid artifacts (furniture, clothing, watches, pens, papers, books) come alive to tell, not a dead story of the past, but a *living story* of the present?

For Tim, it all came together in quite an organic fashion as a result of a special recipe: his *planned* preparation as a historian and an artistic designer, and in his *unplanned* encounters with both. Tim's strong suit of imagination opened his eyes to see more than his eyes could reveal.

Three apparently random encounters opened the right doors for a life-changing adventure.

Chapter 7 – A focus for the museum's "Grand Opening"

Because Tim began his new job in 2018, his first decision was to begin his research with the 100th anniversary of the great flu pandemic beginning in 1918. This seemed a perfectly timed focus for the grand opening of the new museum. But the more he investigated that pandemic, the more he found some very interesting aspects of *another* pandemic, reflected - even focused - in New England's history.

His research generated a series of questions in his mind about how the smallpox pandemic may have affected the inhabitants of the *Yellow House*, the Soule-Seabury family, a prominent fixture of New England and of that very neighborhood known as *Four Corners* in Tiverton. That building, built about 1770 but now fully restored to the 1800s, would become the home of the new museum, so featuring its early inhabitants in a first exhibit was a natural choice.

And New England was filled with interesting stories from that era, especially related to the smallpox pandemic. One, about Benjamin Franklin, caught his attention, even though its roots predated the 1800s. It was about Ben Franklin's changing perspective on the new smallpox inoculation. Historians are always curious about why and how important perceptions change.

Franklin is best known as a Philadelphia resident, but he started his publishing career in his native Boston, working for his older brother. It was also very likely that he and Abner Soule, who first built the *Yellow House*, and who had served in the American Revolutionary Army, had crossed paths.

Exploring how that local family had dealt with the smallpox pandemic was an easy progression, especially because of the very significant connections of the pandemic to that of Boston's becoming a center of medical research, including early treatments for smallpox.

To focus on that story was the first of the three decisions which would change Tim's life; and it was perhaps the most expected.

But the next two were less expected.

While tackling his first objective in his new job, that of archiving the museum's documents and artifacts, he found an entry in a diary from one of the butlers of the Soule-Seabury house about a copy of a book by Washington Irving, *The Sketch Book*, which included "The Legend of Sleepy Hollow." That short story had been published in a magazine in 1819 by itself, without the others in the complete *Sketch Book* collection. That date originally supported the planned opening in 2019, exactly 200 years later. This would be a perfect advertising advantage for the grand opening, especially it were scheduled for around Halloween.

But the first publication in *book form* was in 1820, which added to the historical connection to a 2020 opening. So, Tim actually had a two-year option for promoting an opening in either 2019 or 2020. As it turned out, for financial and administrative reasons, the actual opening season for the exhibit was scheduled for both years: the fall of 2019 through the summer of 2020.

The plan was perfect (whether intentional or accidental) for an anniversary opening related to that story of the *headless horseman*, a New England favorite.

Chapter 8 – A lost book, waiting to be found

The publication date of the Washington Irving book was not referenced in the diary. The diary notation was part of a sequential entry which covered some period of time and from the brief comment, there was no way of knowing about its edition, which was important because there were several printings. But finding that book, regardless of the details, became a priority objective.

The unsolved mystery -- the first of several to follow -- was the question of where the book was in the house, if it even still existed. And if it could be found, Tim wondered if it had fought off mold and insects for over two centuries, if cast aside.

Tim understood the dangers of being cast aside, and being found was not just a professional goal, but a personal one.

So the search became laser-focused in Tim's new personal and professional life -- that of finding and being found.

Chapter 9 – One discovery starts another

Tim's job description involved pursuing both intentional and accidental discoveries of items already in the house (soon to be the museum). He continued the painstaking task of carefully documenting the wide assortment of papers and other artifacts already available for display. Many of the items were directly traceable to Abner Soule or Cornelius Seabury, the resident in 1820.

And then...

The former star quarterback crossed the goal line!

He had found in a dusty, undocumented and unlabeled box, stored away in a back closet, the book probably referenced in the diary. It was long hidden but it was in remarkable condition. Could it be verified to be the same book? Were there any notations that could directly connect the book to the Seabury family, or explain how it got into their hands? And were there any clues as to why it had been hidden for so long?

Handling it carefully, with clean, white, museum-gloves, his discovery led to a huge smile -- the first time he had smiled that much in quite some time. It was the touchdown he had hoped for!

The book itself was nothing short of miraculously historical because it was an original, *first edition copy* of *The Sketch Book*, the one published in 1820 by Washington Irving. This was the collection of stories which included, as described, the very famous "Legend of Sleepy Hollow." According to Britannica, "*The Sketch Book* was a celebrated event in American literary history. The collection was the first American work of short stories to gain international success and popularity."

But there was more...

His internet search could only find a very few first edition copies, all in poorer condition, and yet each one on the market was valued at over $40,000!

And there was even *more*...

This hidden and well-preserved copy was *signed* by Washington Irving himself "To Jane Seabury - October 12, 1820" in Irving's own handwriting!

An internet search could not find evidence of another signed and dated copy, so its value was perhaps limited only by his wildest dreams!

The book, with a direct connection to the Seabury family and to the Soule-Seabury house, could become a national attraction, and for a small, local museum it would be the centerpiece of its first exhibit.

So this unexpected discovery led to a final confirmation of the focus on the year 1820 which would be celebrated during its 200th anniversary in a grand exhibition for the museum in 2020.

Chapter 10 - As in any ghost story, a predictable turn of events: the unpredictable happens

The first serendipitous decision made by Tim was to seek -- and find -- a connection to the right period of history for an opening exhibit, with a direct connection to New England. That process led him beyond the first obvious connection to the flu pandemic to a more intriguing era of a waning smallpox pandemic. It was not the height of the pandemic but in retrospect, the waning years are not known at that time as an end but are experienced as yet another of an unknown number of waves. Investigating how a local family lived during that period would be a contribution to history, and as a historian, Tim liked that challenge. Especially since America had not experienced anything like waves of a pandemic since 1918-1920.

At least, not yet...

That decision was predictable. But...

The second turning point was the accidental discovery of the 1820 signed copy of *The Sketch Book*, with another direct connection to the Yellow House.

The third significant decision was purely accidental ... maybe.

It was a discovery by way of a connection through Terry.

As described earlier, among her old high school classmates was Abby, a local artist who had a fairly successful but still struggling art store. She had recently decided to venture into sculpture but working with wood and stone proved to be quite challenging, so she started creating wax figures. This actually helped her business in a very practical way, not so much to the artistic community, but to the business community. There were several local shops which needed to display clothes and hats and shoulder strap purses and more, all enhanced by creatively designed wax figures.

One afternoon, walking from the museum on his way to have dinner with Terry and her family, Tim passed by a store with one of Abby's decorated and well clothed wax figures. He was surprised to discover that the very real-looking figures featured moveable part at every joint, which his exhibit design back in Philadelphia could not manage. And, even better, they were quite affordable.

He had entered the store to purchase something for Terry but wound up buying a new idea: the historical persona of his exhibit would become locally crafted wax figures, all dressed in period attire! And the costumes could be sewn by Suzie's dress shop. And all artistically photographed for the displays by his high school classmate, Robert.

The strength of a support system became even more obvious.

So, by chance, the new exhibit had been shaped by an anniversary, a dusty closet surprise, and an accidental encounter with a window display. These unplanned events turned out to be central to our story, and to Tim's story.

But were they truly unplanned? Or were they coordinated, or at least fostered, by.....

Alas, we are getting ahead of the story...

Chapter 11-- The museum curator: director of marketing

Since the museum was located in a well-known house built in the heart of Four Corners, Tim convinced the trustees to have a major exhibit featuring the prominent family who lived there. The records were incomplete, but apparently the house had been painted a bright yellow from its original construction around 1770, and it was still yellow when plans for the museum were drafted. The building was commonly referred to as, simply, the *Yellow House.*

Tim made a good first impression with his marketing strategy by way of three important suggestions.

First, the name of the museum should be changed from the initial, more formal and uninviting *Museum of Four Corners*, to the more informal and inviting *Museum of the Yellow House,* which would encourage curiosity in search for an interesting story-filled find.

The second marketing suggestion was the decision to focus on the 1820 connection to *The Sketch Book*, a perfect advertising advantage for the exhibit. His ability to connect the dots with flexibility, from an original concept to a new one, made quite an impression on the museum's trustees.

And the third suggestion was an adaptation from his experience in Philadelphia. He suggested a contest among the artisans of Four Corners to create contributing aspects of wax figures and costumes for four Seabury family members who lived in the house during that period: Cornelius, a prominent businessman of that era, and a direct descendent of Abner; Mary, his wife; and Jane and Benjamin, two of their 12 children. The winners of the competition would benefit from free advertising, including a mention in the exhibit brochure, two plaques (one displayed at the exhibit and one at the artist's studio), and as an added benefit, a perpetual family pass to all museum exhibits.

As a trained historian and designer of museum presentations, Tim now shifted to a focus on the historical and cultural context of his planned exhibit in order to develop a full story for the museum's guests.

The background for an appealing exhibit was now ready to be fully operationalized, and perhaps it was also ready to renew hope for Tim and his career.

Chapter 12 -- The Abner Soule story

Abner Soule, a direct descendent of George Soule and a passenger of the original Mayflower's journey to America, was born on March 27, 1748 in Tiverton, RI, at a time when the American colonies were moving toward independence. Abner was a classic symbol of early American history: he served in the Colonial Army during the American War of Independence; he was a hard working blacksmith and a New England whaler; and he and his wife had 12 children, a common family size in early America.

Such a representative figure in both our local and national history, Abner would also be a good choice for a side exhibit.

Chapter 13 -- The *Yellow House*

Though Tim found the records to be incomplete, the common oral history described the building's yellow paint from its very beginning, around 1770.

The house was deeded to Abner's son, Cornelius in 1808. Cornelius was also a classic symbol of the American entrepreneurs of the era: a sea captain, farmer, politician and a merchant in the China trade. He was even associated with John Jacob Astor's effort to build a fur-trading empire in the Pacific Northwest.

In 1809, Cornelius remodeled the house, creating the Federal style that is visible today.

In 1816, Cornelius Soule deeded the house as payment for accrued debts, to his cousin, Cornelius Seabury, "Little" George's father in the family central to the exhibit. Only two years later, in 1818, Cornelius Soule died at sea, while on a merchant ship.

A museum curator could not hope for a more interesting New England family history.

Chapter 14 -- The Soule-Seabury
family history

After delving into the background history of the Soule-Seabury family for the new exhibit, Tim found an appealing and touching story -- a story whose depth he never fully knew even though he grew up in Four Corners. That was a lesson itself: a local boy who came home to find himself also began to find others, past and present, as he saw his own village with fresh eyes.

The first child of Cornelius and Mary Seabury was George Seabury, probably named for another George, the more famous and extremely respected George *Washington*, who was serving as the new nation's first President at the time of the baby's birth, in 1795. Or perhaps he was named for his ancestor, George Soule, the passenger on the Mayflower, bringing English settlers to New England. Or both.

With the plausibility of either reason for his name, Tim decided to create the nickname *Little George*, who became a larger-than-life focus of the exhibit. As far as Tim knew, based on available records, diaries and folklore, he was the first to apply that moniker.

Despite the strength and depth of his family tree, a very young George Seabury died after living only two weeks, during a period in American history when the smallpox pandemic was still fostering fear, in spite of a revolutionary, new vaccine. There was no medical record indicating that George was a victim of smallpox, but it would have been possible, and it most certainly would have been on the family's minds, adding to their fear of the future.

Tim also tracked a trail of ghost stories in the town's folklore and oral history, about Little George's haunting the Yellow House. He did recall hearing some of these as a child, but he now had a greater appreciation for the role of ghost stories in the lives of families facing fear, then and now. This would also be the focus of a side exhibit.

Chapter 15 -- The Smallpox

The mystery and uncontrollable power of disease has haunted humanity for millennia, and the American colonies and fledging nation were not exempt.

Many diseases threatened families in the era of this new exhibit. Tim found a 1735 article in the *Boston Globe* which reported that a village in New Hampshire experienced 32% of deaths from diphtheria among children under 10. But smallpox was something different; it was a worldwide pandemic with a long history and Americans came to know the illness personally, as they directly experienced the fear that smallpox stirred.

And Tim discovered that Boston was at the center of both the swirling fear and the slow acceptance of the successful prevention of smallpox.

While the use of inoculation, the predecessor to a vaccine, traces back through centuries in Africa, a Boston minister, none other than Cotton Mather, learned of the practice through one of his African slaves, Onesimus, a named assigned by his master from that of a slave in the Bible.

The circumstances of that discovery reveals our complex American history regarding slavery: Mather apparently beat the information out of his slave. Sadly the hidden contributions of slaves and the abusive manipulation of their advanced cultural wisdom is not generally known, much less acknowledged. Tim found it interesting that most accounts of Mather's "learning" describe Onesimus as simply "giving" this information, an oversimplification and a "white-washing" of the events. But, *that* is another story...

After a smallpox outbreak in 1721, Mather convinced a Boston doctor, Zabdiel Boylston, to spread the word about the effectiveness of the practice. Boylston inoculated two of his African slaves (one of whom was only 2 years old) and his own son, who was 6 at the time. In that act, Boston became the site of the first use of an inoculation in North America.

The result: even though the treatment was effective, Boylston was met with violent threats.

Always viewing the past through the lens of a historian, Tim wondered if, in the unlikely scenario of a new pandemic affecting

America, would there be a repeated battle between information and misinformation. Would history rhyme again?

Tim preferred to place these uncomfortable thoughts on a mental shelf in a back closet, especially since a similar scenario would be very unlikely to occur in a modern America.

But the story of Ben Franklin's view on inoculations stirred some second thoughts.

Franklin was but a teen when he started working for his older brother, James, as an apprentice in the publishing world. James was an avid anti-inoculation spokesman and he more than allowed, even encouraged, articles in his *New England Courier* to support his view.

James influenced his younger brother, Ben, who became a partner in publishing misinformation about the safety and effectiveness of the inoculation treatment.

Until...

Benjamin's own son died in 1736 of smallpox at age 4. Reflecting on this later, in his 1771 *Autobiography*, he noted his "bitter regret" that he had not allowed his son to be inoculated. His changed view was likely influenced by a post-publishing career in science, a field which valued the weighing of observable evidence and a "cost/benefit" assessment before reaching conclusions, rather than relying on campaigns of misinformation.

And in the present first decades of the 21st Century, history did seem to be in a rhyme.

That led to Tim's decision to design a side exhibit on the *scientific method* to offer a contrast to modern examples of approaches to decision-making which *avoided* evidence-based research. It was an effort to present the many sides of how one could approach the investigation of controversial issues, then and now. In addition, another exhibit would present a timeline of both *fear* (a key factor in misinformation) and the *resolution* of the smallpox pandemic (a key factor in hope). The historian in him wanted to address the existence of both fact and fiction in the midst of a frightening experience.

While some of the museum trustees were, themselves, uncomfortable with these dynamics of the 1700's and 1800s, and reluctant to openly address any controversial topics by way of additional exhibits, Tim was able to present a convincing case for historical accuracy. "Honesty and transparency in the face of fear is empowering," he argued. "And those who ignore the past will never find its lessons."

Returning to his research, Tim learned that in 1777, during the American War of Independence, George Washington, then Commander of the Continental Army, required all recruits to be inoculated. Similar requirements were later made by town and state legislatures and supported by court reviews.

1796, the year after *Little George's* death, the English physician, Edward Jenner, gave his new vaccine successfully to a first subject, an 8-year old child, but it wasn't until 1820 (another interesting connection to the overall focus of the museum's opening) that London saw the beginning of a decrease in the number of deaths from smallpox.

In 1800, a Harvard professor of medicine, Benjamin Waterhouse, gave the first vaccine in America, to his own children. The vaccine was successful, but there was still resistance to its use, even then.

That resistance continued even while the

smallpox pandemic was beginning to fade by the early 1800s, with the impact of the new vaccine.

Tim began to consider a new perspective on trends over time -- perhaps for *every* time -- which could enlighten his understanding of behaviors at every level of life -- political, professional, and even personal.

Perhaps anything, and everything, exists somewhere along a spectrum -- a continuum -- between the two primary emotions in life: fear and hope.

That theory would certainly apply to history, and even to his own struggle between those extremes, sometimes swinging like a pendulum, awaiting, and hoping for its own calm rest-stop.

As for his new exhibit, he knew that the fear of death by disease was still a powerful cloud over the Soule-Seabury house in 1820.

Little did Tim realize how prophetic the exhibit would be, when seen with the perspective of 2020...

Chapter 16 – The Grand Opening

Pat, Terry's husband and the local police chief, bought a dozen helium-filled balloons and banners, for the occasion.

Grand Guy – Grand Opening

Grand Opening by a Grand Director

Welcoming the Past into the Present

*Open the Door to the Past
and a Window to the Future*

Tim was at the top of his mountain, finally... and *again*, like the old days.

With Terry's help, flyers and posters were printed and distributed throughout the Four Corners neighborhood. Thanks to their combined network of friends, word spread by way of news releases and, of course, the ever-powerful and historically dependable *word-of-mouth*.

The official opening day was scheduled for Halloween, 2019.

The national economy was secure, the crime rates were down, and opportunities for local growth seemed promising, as did the ticket sales...for the first few months.

Tim had put his *all* into his first museum season, in a hopeful step-up in his career. With his innovations imported from the big city, the opening had gone well. To assure its success, he spent extra hours every day checking and re-checking each exhibit, and occasionally updating any interpretive signage, to keep up with any current events relative to the displays.

With the Seabury family room at the center, each tour began there and ended there, with much of the antique furniture and fixtures from the early 1800s strategically placed. Tim had even used some of his discovered diary entries from maids and butlers to assist in the arrangement of the room. Everything in the house had been refurbished or carefully replaced using period tools and even period recipes for paint and stains.

The wax figures were placed in that family room, each in period attire (accurate to the buttons!), and each with a welcoming smile and position.

The side rooms were used for the smaller, more specialized and focused exhibits.

Tim's creativity -- and even his attention to detail, the more challenging goal for him to achieve -- had risen to new heights.

And in an effort to be more independent and not impose on Terry, he converted an unused storage closet at the museum into a small studio apartment. It was cramped, but at least he was making it on his own, a value imbedded in his upbringing.

His careful research and innovative ideas about both marketing and exhibit design brought an unexpected number of visitors. There were newspaper and radio reports, including interviews with his former classmates, Carol and Ann. He was beginning to find himself, again. His efforts were paying off.

Until...

the coronavirus pandemic.

Chapter 17 – A Grand Closing

After a successful beginning, the museum significantly limited its exhibits due to the Covid-19 pandemic.

Every employee and volunteer worked hard to try to save the venture with an innovative effort to offer special opportunities for single-family tours or small school tours by individual classrooms. With Terry's help, they even offered virtual tours.

But the expense of the enhanced technology, even with Terry's discounts, and special stepped–up cleanings, only added to the already budgeted and consistent costs of utilities and maintenance.

The spring of 2020 hit a pandemic height but by the summer, the situation seemed to improve. Even so, after the summer "recess" of the virus, a new wave appeared in the fall. Facing mounting debts, the trustees planned to auction off the museum's copy of Washington Irving's *Sketch Book*, to meet the budget.

The pandemic had brought an additional fear to the already heavy weight on Tim's shoulders. It was another chance that he

could be cast aside again, especially with the
trustee's consideration of a shut-down. And
his likelihood of being even *more* dependent
on Terry stirred a renewed fear of failure.

He now faced an over-arching fear beyond
finding a new career -- would he find a new
life -- of any kind?

His pendulum was still swinging between
fear and hope, when, on a crisp autumn
evening, when sunset was late enough to
keep the stars at bay, something changed.

It was Halloween night, October 31, 2020.

It all started in plain sight, though Tim
couldn't see it.

PART 2: THE PRESENT

Chapter 18 – The last tour of the season, and a mystery visitor arrives

By early fall, businesses everywhere and of all types were cutting back, as the reality of a new wave (foreshadowing an unknown cycle) began to sink in. After a difficult year, the trustees decided to take a break, closing its first season around Halloween, in 2020, with an unpredictable timing for a reopening.

Tim had resigned himself, as much as he could, to an uncertain future, but typical for extraverts, when under stress, they become even more expressive, so Tim led his last known tour that night with exceptional energy.

But for an extravert, *hiding* the inner fears was a challenge. Extraverts have very little filter between brain and mouth, so it was hard to store his state of mind inside both brain and lips. If a perfect stranger asked the right question, he might begin to verbally spill the entire story, especially to someone who was a good listener.

But that was not his role on this performance day, the last tour of the season.

Leading a tour is like doing Community Theater – and one needs to prepare for the role internally. He needed to hide those inner worries and put on a "happy face" for the museum visitors. After all, they were supporting the community efforts during troubled times and they deserved a pleasant experience.

At the museum, it was the last tour of the last evening before the first season's end.

It had taken the visitors through each room of the Yellow House, passing by the wax figures of the Seabury family several times: Cornelius, the stately father-figure; Mary, his quite proper-looking wife; Benjamin, one of their sons; and Jane, one of their younger daughters. All were sharply costumed in period attire, with careful attention to every detail. Even the buttons on the shirts and dresses were designed from a pattern taken from authentic samples from a Boston museum.

The tour went smoothly. No one asked a question that couldn't be answered, nor did anyone ask a question which would have opened the flood gates of Tim's thoughts. And the first season of the new museum had, somehow, made it to its closure in the fall of 2020.

Now standing next to the wax figures, Tim offered a final observation as the tourists gathered near the door of the exhibition area.

By this moment, he and the guests both understood, cognitively and emotionally, how some of the exhibits had been eerie premonitions.

His final speech to the visitors was partly a summary of what they had seen in the exhibits and partly a final reference to one of the more sentimental characters of the house's story – that of "Little George."

"And the family member to remind you about, is *Little George,* the first child of Mary and Cornelius. You may have walked right by his tombstone in the family cemetery on the way into the museum, but you probably didn't notice the birth and death dates on the marker: he died at the very young age of only two weeks, just before the turn of the century, in 1795, when George *Washington* was President."

"I encourage you to pause there on the way out, to reflect on their grief and their loss of hope in that tragedy. But keep in mind that the generation of the American Revolution was resilient. And the Soule-Seabury family moved beyond that crisis to become an established and well-to-do family of Four Corners, right here in Tiverton, with businesses here and also in Newport and even in Boston."

"Some people have speculated that, because of his tragic death, Little George became the *Ghost of the Yellow House* who has haunted the estate for over 200 years. Mysterious and unexplained things *have* happened here, but, then again, no one knows whether those have been caused by ghosts or by scientific phenomena. We'll never know for sure – and, well, many people today don't even believe in ghosts any more. They may be, as historians would describe it, a relic of the past."

"Now, as we bring our tour and our season to an end here at the *Museum of the Yellow House*, let us thank the members of the Soule-Seabury family, represented by their wax figures, for sharing the story of their lives, as they lived them, exactly 200 years ago, in the autumn of 1820!"

After a brief silence, the small group of gathered tourists looked at each other and simultaneously joined into a gentle applause. Tim graciously bowed, ever so slightly, to the sound of "Thank you! Very interesting! Good job!"

Then Tim could not resist one of his home-made proverbs:

"I don't know who said it first, but 'Time flies when you are learning from history!'"

And then a parting and timely final word, with a grin:

"Some of you may have noticed this morning's red sky, just before dawn. Recall the old saying, 'Red sky at night, museum visitor's delight; red sky in the morning, museum visitor's warning.' Since it *is* Halloween, don't let the *Ghost of the Yellow House* catch you off guard!"

The tourists chuckled and then formed a single line as they exited, while Tim was momentarily distracted, looking for some notes he had made that day about some changes for the next season's displays.

Having left the door open, a stranger found his way in.

But not a stranger anyone would have expected.

The stranger was dressed in period attire from head to toe, perfectly matching the costumes of the commissioned wax figures of the Soule-Seabury family. How he had known about their exact appearance remains a mystery, still to this day. Perhaps he had visited the museum before or perhaps he had seen one of the publicity photos. Perhaps he had some mysterious "insider information". He even had some make-up that made him look "waxy", so he could easily blend in with the family of wax figures.

Which is exactly what he did, quickly and quietly taking a pose at the end of the family line-up, taking in a deep breath and freezing. He was hoping Tim wouldn't notice him, since he was in a hurry to find his notes, lock up the museum for the night and for the season, and then make a quick exit.

But walking back to close the door, Tim paused, sensing that something had changed. His first response was to feel a chill at the base of his skull – an unconscious acknowledgment of the fast approaching Halloween night, there, completely alone in a house haunted by the presence of a 200 year old ghost.

Next, his physical sensation of smell combined with his intuition, caught his attention. His normal personality style was to notice what was *missing* in a scene (which contributed to his creative imagination), but for once, he began to focus not on what was missing, but on what was *added* to the room.

He glanced through the family room to see if any chairs had been moved, or if something else about the room was different. Then he turned his attention to the wax figures. As he briskly walked past their row, something did seem out-of-place. The first signal was that there was now an *odd* number of figures (5), though there had earlier been an *even* number of figures (4, only Cornelius, Mary, Benjamin and Jane).

And then there was the whiff of "waxy make-up" that also added to the assembly of characters.

He retraced his steps along the line of family figures, pausing like a general reviewing the troops before a military engagement of great import. Each figure received a close look, from toe to head. Slowly, past each family member, they all passed inspection, and as Tim moved on past the newest member of the troops, that figure let out and then breathed in a quick-but-not-so silent breath. And that's when Tim paused to back up, just in time to catch the figure in motion.

"Where did *you* come from?" he asked, in a gruff and demanding voice. And then, in a tone of curiosity, "And more important, *who* are you?"

The uninvited visitor had been caught, and he had to think fast.

The figure now spoke, quickly coming up with an excuse for sneaking in. "Uh...I am actually... an *actor*, practicing my ability to pose like a wax figure."

Tim was not buying it, and his silent stare spoke very loudly.

Speedily, sensing the urgent need to add to his explanation, the figure continued. "...And, uh, I happen to be a *descendent* of Cornelius Seabury. I'm preparing for a part in a play about his life, and I thought this would be a great place to practice my *method* acting...you know, seeing and breathing the life of the character."

"Well, *whoever* you are…"

"…Jack. The name is Jack."

Now in a tone somewhere between anger and a lecture, Tim continued. "Jack, this is NOT a theater. It is a *museum* -- a sacred space where *history* is celebrated, and, to be sure, *honored.*"

"Well then", came a rapid response. "We are *both* in luck. Because I am *also* a student of history. I've been reading up on this, uh, *my*, family history."

And in an effort to further convince Tim of his sincerity, "Just test me - give me a *Soule-Seabury Family History Quiz!*"

"OK, I'll do just that..." And a rapid-fire Q&A began. "Who built the Yellow House at Four Corners?"

"Abner Soule."

"Who was Abner Soule?"

"A blacksmith, a direct descendant of a Mayflower passenger, a Revolutionary War hero, and a whaler."

"Who was Cornelius Soule?"

"Abner's son."

"When did Cornelius Soule deed the house to his cousin, Cornelius Seabury?"

"1816."

"How many children did Cornelius Seabury and his wife, Mary, have?"

"12."

"What was the name of the 1st of their 12 children?"

"George, who was born one year after they were married, and who, sadly, died after living only two weeks."

After a pause, a bit surprised but pleased, Tim's breathing shifted from tense to relaxed, as he admitted, "Wow, you passed the test -- with flying colors! I'm quite impressed with your knowledge-- and your apparent appreciation of the history -- the one thing that has always given me hope."

After a pause which hinted, for the first time, the internal tug of a festering fear, he added, "Until now..."

"Until now? Tell me more. I'm a good listener…"

Jack was, in fact, **not** a good listener, though he **was** a good liar. And as a good actor, and a very self-centered one, he could *act* like a listener -- a skill he developed because it often fed his egocentrism and got him what he wanted.

After a pause to think about how much of his story he wanted to share, Tim began what sounded like the start of a confession before a priest.

"Well…it all began when I became the curator here, with a chance to open a new museum. I thought I had a golden opportunity to start a new career. I scheduled a grand opening, with these specially commissioned wax figures, and it must have been my fate to schedule it at the same time as the *grand opening* of a new pandemic."

"I can guess the rest."

"People didn't want to get out and about, and we had to cut back on the number of tickets we could sell. All the costs were the same, but even with virtual tours our income has dropped so much, the museum is about to close down."

Still acting in his new role as a priest, pretending to listen with empathy, Jack responded, "That's awful."

"Oh, but it gets worse."

"Worse?"

"As a part of our grand opening we were going to display an autographed, First Edition copy of *The Sketch Book* from exactly 200 years ago, 1820."

Now, Jack was listening intensely, leaning on every word Tim was about to share, as he demonstrated his literary awareness. "The book by Washington Irving, which included "The Legend of Sleepy Hollow?"

"The same. And if we had to, because of the pandemic, we could sell the book in order to save the museum. But for some reason, the book has disappeared...As has any sense of hope -- for the museum, or for *me*."

Jack's mind was somewhere between shocked and puzzled as he responded, in his priestly, therapeutic role, repeating Tim's confession, in Rogerian fashion, "I hear you saying the book has *disappeared*."

Trying to make sense of what doesn't make sense, Tim tried to be rational. "Oh, we think it's still somewhere in the museum. It's hard to explain, but things in here sometimes mysteriously move around for no apparent reason. So, we suspect that's what's happened to the book."

"Things just move around, mysteriously?"

"Strange, isn't it? Especially at this time of the year, around Halloween."

Still in the priestly role, "I wish I could help. Wait…wait. I *may* be able to help, after all. Perhaps my theater group could put on a play about the Soule-Seabury family, as a fund raiser?"

For the first time in weeks, naively sensing an unexpected gift from an unknown source, bringing the appearance of a brief ray of light and hope onto a dark and frightful night, Tim thought out loud, "Perhaps you can..."

He looked at his watch and continued, "Listen, I have to meet my sister, Terry, and her family for dinner, but, I'll tell you what. I'll let you stay here for an hour or so, getting in touch with the 'inner soul' of your '*Soule*-Seabury character' -- get it?"

Tim and Jack both shared a smile as Tim had a premonition that he may have found more than hope -- a new friend he could trust.

"…and then I'll be back to talk more and lock up the museum for the season."

"Oh, thank you so much, ah, ah…"

"Tim…" And looking at his watch he continued, "Ok, let's see, it's 6:15, I'll be back at, say, 7:30."

He headed toward the door where he stopped to say, in a very serious tone, "Oh….be *very* careful, and ***don't touch anything***!"

Jack was quick to respond in an affirming, "Oh, you have my word!"

But once Tim left the museum, Jack immediately grabbed his cell phone and after dialing, started to go through papers on a desk with the other hand. To anyone who could have seen it, the image of a liar and a con-man was transparent.

"Jill? I'm in – it's a good thing we rehearsed the family history."

Someone on the other end of the line had answered, "I figured you'd be quizzed if you got caught. And I'll bet that information about Little George's death, after living only two weeks, was the clincher."

"You were right. But now, we have to move fast."

The response came in a slightly condescending voice, "Don't we have all night, like I planned it?"

"No, I'll explain later. The curator will be back at 7:30." Then after a brief pause, "So, what have you got?"

"OK, according to the museum website, the signed, First Edition copy of Washington Irving's *Sketch Book*, published in 1820, will be on display. Try looking on a mantle, or in a bookcase -- *everywhere*. And call me when you find it."

Jack ended the call, and something quite unexpected happened.

The wax figures came to life!

And the first one to speak was Cornelius, in a matter-fact manner, directed to Jack.

"Oh, Charles, I'm glad you came in from feeding the animals in the stable. We need some firewood for the wood stove. It's going to be a tad chilly tonight."

Jack was frozen with fear – and questions. Why did a dead wax figure from 200 years ago suddenly come to life? And how? And why did he think Jack was a stable-boy named Charles?

Still in shock, Jack spoke not a word. So Cornelius filled the silence, in a lecture-style voice. "Now, Charles. That *is* a part of your job, as the stable boy. Be a good lad, and fetch the wood. We also need a good fire tonight because we're going to have a special family hour, first playing our weekly riddle game from a new riddle-book I found at the book dealer near my Newport office. It's so new, the book dealer next to my office here in Four Corners didn't have it."

Jack was still speechless -- as silent and frozen as the wax figures had been only moments before.

Cornelius continued, "Then, a special reading from *another* new book."

The father figure then quickly fell into a comfortable routine (at least for the historical figures). "First, for Jane, here is your weekly test of problem-solving skills: What goes from Newport to Boston without moving?"

There was silence for a beat, and then Jane answered, "I don't have any idea."

"A road!"

"Oh, Father. That one was too tricky!"

Cornelius continued. "All right, then, try this one: What is the smallest bridge in the world?"

"One over a small stream? Oh, a bridge in a musical score?"

"No. The bridge on your nose!" After the sound of sighs, Cornelius moved quickly to the next, "Now, another one: what has a neck but no head?"

Again, silence for a beat.

"A shirt!"

After another round of sighs from both Jane and Mary, and even from Benjamin, who had been quietly listening, as a true introvert would in a group, Cornelius continued, "Next, a personal puzzle: if you had a choice, would you choose to be deaf or blind?"

Jane quickly responded to this one, with enthusiastic energy, "That's easy! To be deaf."

Mary finally spoke up, "Why, my child?"

"Because being blind would make it harder to read. And speaking of reading, can we get on with the reading from the new book? I *love* new books!"

Mary added this to the family gathering: "I agree. Because the book is a special surprise."

"Really?" Jane asked, her curiosity now peaked.

Eager to offer an explanation, Mary added, "Since your birthday is fast approaching, and since we all know how much you like books, when I heard that the book dealer next to your Father's *Boston* office was having a special sale of a brand new book, *The Sketch Book*...well, I made sure to be there."

Jack, now Charles, had been listening (for a change) and with each mention of the word "book," he showed an increased interest.

Jane nearly jumped with surprise. "Wait. You mean the book which includes 'The Legend of Sleepy Hollow'? My teacher has talked about that story!"

"Yes, my child. *And*, I was able to buy a copy of the book, signed by the author himself! I knew that was the best gift I could buy for you."

"Oh, Mother! How special!"

Cornelius, still absorbing this new information, asked, "You mean, the great Washington Irving *himself*, signed the book?"

"Yes, indeed. And I brought it home and hid it in a very safe place, to be sure no one would find it and spoil the surprise!"

Jack now dived into the conversation; after all, he desperately wanted that book, to please his partner in crime. In a rapid pace, he asked, "Where is it?"

Once he realized the shocked expressions around him, he quickly backed away, adding, to avoid suspicion, "I mean... how...how clever of you to hide it so well."

Cornelius chimed in with his typically logical observation, "You know, some day that book may be quite valuable. I would hide it *very well*. In these hard times, one has to be on constant guard against robbers and thieves. One has to truly fear the sneaky and the selfish, who seem ever on the rise these days. It's not like the old days, when…"

At that point, Mary interrupted with her own typical interpersonal world-view. "Oh, stop, Cornelius. You're always worrying about things that don't last and are not of *real* value. You should be worrying about life and death, hopes and dreams, in spite of fears."

"All right, dear. This sounds like a topic for a later discussion, when we are alone," adding a silent nod toward Jane and Benjamin. And then, "Now, we'll get back to the book…but, first..." he paused to look at his gold pocket watch, a gift from Abner, "...it's tea time."

Jack was taking all of this in, and he knew he had to report on his progress. So he slowly moved to a corner of the family room to dial a number on his cell.

Prepared to whisper when the call was answered, another surprise added a twist to the night's events: with another person on the line, the wax figures froze in place.

When the call went through, he still whispered. "Mom?"

"Don't ever call me 'Mom' on this line. Someone could be listening!"

"Oh, right. But there's no one here but frozen wax figures, at least not now. But the reason for my call is – well, have *I* got news for *you*!"

"I'm listening," came the response.

"Well, the first thing you'll believe: I am about to find the book!" And after a brief pause, "And the second thing, you *won't* believe: this place is...well... *pretty spooky.*

Because…well…I think there are some ghosts in here."

In a strong, lecture-like tone, came, "Jack, don't freak out on me just because it's Halloween. There are no such things as ghosts. Now, get a grip, get off the phone, and *get the book!*"

After a beat, very condescendingly, much more so than before, came, "Oh, and if there *are* any ghosts, maybe they'll help you find it! Ha!"

When the call ended, the wax figures again found life, and began to prepare for tea.

Jack decided to try an experiment. He dialed Jill again, and once more, when the call was answered, the wax figures froze.

From the phone came a surprised Jill: "Did you find it *already*?"

Jack hung up and the wax figures began to move again. So he dialed his mom again.

"Jack, what's going on?"

Jack hung up, again. And then he even repeated these calls to be sure his experiment worked.

Now knowing that he had a way to control the wax figures, his last call was to report his progress - and his plan. Jill finally got a word in. "Jack, quit playing games. I'm on a serious mission here!"

"So am I....*So am I....*"

At last, Jack spoke confidently to his mother. "I have a plan. I'll explain later."

After hanging up on this call, at least for now, the wax figures resumed their evening tea. They moved about until Jack dialed again. As they expectedly froze, Jack continued his phone conversation.

"Don't say anything, just keep this phone line open. I'm going to search for the book."

The wax figures were now in frozen-mode as if electronically set in place, and Jack began to search the room. He looked in the drawers of a desk, on a mantle above the fireplace, and in a nearby bookcase but he found no sign of the book.

He then remembered that Cornelius had a valuable gold pocket watch, and he removed it from Cornelius' helpless figure.

Then he spoke on the open phone line, "Jill, I am still searching. I'll call you back."

Once he ended the call and the wax figures expectedly came alive again, Jack resumed his new role as "Charles," in hope of finding the valuable book...and finally earning his mother's respect.

He looked to Cornelius and respectfully said, "I'll be right back with the firewood, sir," then exited, to begin his search in another room.

The wax figures were now free to talk and walk about, since there were no humans in the room, or no strange new tools, apparently called a "phone line."

Then, another twist to the story unfolded.

Mary went to the bookcase, where *The Sketch Book* had been hidden.

"Here is the book...hidden...*in plain sight.* "

"Like *many* important things," Cornelius observed.

"I put a false book-cover on it to disguise it!" explained Mary, as she held it up, to share a distinct, quilt-like fake cover. She was quite creative with her quilts and she had some unused scraps of material left over from a recent gift to a neighbor. Without removing the cover, she handed it to Cornelius. Mary added, "I think it's time for story-telling, Father."

By now, Jane was beyond her limit of patience. "Oh, yes, Father. Please read the part about the *headless horseman*. I need a scary story to share with the other children at church."

Surprised by her request, Mary asked, "At church! Why?"

"Because of *All Hallows Een*."

Mary and Cornelius gave Jane a puzzled look, and they both spoke at the same time, with two different questions. "What?" and "Why?"

Jane enjoyed every opportunity she had for a role reversal in which she could play the "teaching parent." She smiled before patiently sharing her church lesson.

"A long time ago, people believed that the devil would try to steal the souls -- otherwise known as the ghosts of the saints from their graves, on the eve of a special day to celebrate the saints, commonly known as *All Saints Day*, but also known as *All Hallow's Day*. In order to protect the saints on All Hallow's Eve -- or *All Hallow's Een*, which became *Halloween* -- people would dress up in scary costumes. Scary enough to scare the devil away from the cemetery. So...we are having a contest to see who has the scariest story and costume this year."

Cornelius gave Mary a doubting look, and shared his very old-fashioned perspective on church matters. "I've been telling you that the new priest is introducing some strange ideas from his so-called 'progressive' seminary education."

And Mary crisply responded with, "And *I've* been telling you that our child is very smart for her age."

Jane wanted to refocus the conversation on the book. "Is 'The Legend of Sleepy Hollow' about a *religious* Hollow?" she asked, in her innocent curiosity.

"A different word, my dear."

"Well, is the part about the *headless horseman* spooky? Because a crisp, cool autumn night like tonight is such a good time for a scary story."

But after thinking about that for a moment, she added, "As long as it isn't *too* scary…"

"Oh, my child, this story is more about finding true treasures than it is about ghosts," he reassuringly answered.

"I don't understand."

"Well, let's see..." Thinking of how best to answer this question, he went on, "Let me summarize the heart of the story by way of an introduction."

Jane, along with Mary, and also Benjamin, who characteristically had played his role as the quiet listener, all settled into a comfortable place, mentally and physically, ready to hear this special story.

He continued. "Ichabod Crane was a schoolteacher who came to a place called Sleepy Hollow. He was smart but also tricky, as he courted Katrina, the daughter of the wealthiest farmer in the village. In her, Ichabod had found a true treasure, and he wanted to steal her away from another man, named Brom."

"Now, Brom didn't have the schooling that Ichabod had, but he was clever enough to scare Ichabod away. And Ichabod was afraid that he would lose his true treasure."

Jane interrupted with a question. "How did Brom do that? And why was Ichabod afraid?"

"Let's do some reading to find out," her father responded.

While Cornelius was turning the pages of the book to find a good starting point, Jack entered the room with the firewood. As he stacked the wood near the fireplace, he listened without asking more questions, a challenge for an extreme extravert, but one he accepted, given the potential benefit: to get his hands on the book.

Having found the right place to begin, Cornelius continued. "This passage describes Sleepy Hollow:"

Reading from the book, and at times, offering his own commentary...

"Here the author describes the fall season, just as Ichabod saw it…"

Now reading, "It was…a fine autumnal day; the sky was clear and serene…The forests had put on their sober brown and yellow, while some trees of the tenderer kind had been nipped by the frosts into brilliant dyes of orange, purple, and scarlet. Streaming files of wild ducks began to make their appearance high in the air; the bark of the squirrel might be heard from the groves of beech and hickory-nuts, and the pensive whistle of the quail at intervals from the neighboring field."

Then, an interjected commentary, "Now, it was into this village of Sleepy Hollow that Ichabod became the schoolmaster, a position which was, as the author writes, here…"

"…of some importance in the female circle of a rural neighborhood; being considered a kind of idol."

He went on to read that Ichabod "was esteemed by the women as a man of great erudition, for he had read several books, quite through, and was a perfect master of Cotton Mather's *History of New England Witchcraft*, in which, by the way, he most firmly and potently believed."

"Ichabod was, in fact, an odd mixture of small shrewdness and simple credulity. Another of his sources of fearful pleasure was to pass long winter evenings with the old Dutch wives, as they sat spinning by the fire, with a row of apples roasting and spluttering along the hearth, and listen to their marvelous tales of ghosts..."

He then began to slow down and build to his "scary voice" for a dramatic effect, something Cornelius enjoyed doing whenever reading for the children.

"...and goblins...and haunted fields...and haunted brooks...and haunted bridges...and haunted houses...and *particularly* of the *headless horseman.*"

Jane could not control her excitement, "Oh, Mother, this is beginning to sound like a good ghost story! Read more about the *headless horseman*, Father."

Knowing that he had captured Jane's full attention, Cornelius continued. "It is said by some to be the ghost of a Hessian trooper, whose head had been carried away by a cannon-ball, in some nameless battle during the Revolutionary War."

"But why did the *headless horseman* appear in the story?" Jane blurted out.

Cornelius slowed down his pace, and in a calm voice, answered, "We'll get to that...

Chapter 19 – The eyes now see

When Tim left the museum, he was completely blind to the con he fell for.

Lots of things can make us figuratively blind: insecurity, fear, over-trusting as well as under-trusting, to mention only a few.

While sitting at her dining room table, a computer nearby, his eyes were unexpectedly opened in this expected visit.

Tim had entered Terry's house, shivering a bit, after a long walk from the museum in the night cold. Greeting his sister, he expectedly shared one of his original sayings. "Hi, Terry. Gosh, it's as cold as a wi…err... a ghost's nose."

"Be careful, Tim. Don't say anything bad about a ghost on Halloween. It might come back to haunt you."

"I didn't think of the timing for that joke. You may be right."

They both got a laugh out of it, this time not as a response to his unique sayings but simply for the humor of the moment.

Terry was the one who returned them to one item on the agenda for their meeting. "And speaking of Halloween, I finished mending the costume you wore last year. I think it's still worth using." Tim surveyed the contents of a large box which held his costume, and blurted out, "Fantastic! It looks great!"

Noticing for the first time that Pat, Terry's husband, and their son, also Tim (named after his uncle) were not there, he asked, "Say, where is everybody?"

"Pat and *Little Tim* aren't home yet from the away game".

Tim explained that he had asked Pat to do some research for him, but they hadn't seen each other to discuss it.

"I'm not surprised, since you both have had such busy schedules lately. You at the museum all hours of the day and night, and Pat with his Police Chief duties, keeping tabs on all the usual Halloween pranks."

Terry's cell phone rang.

"Oh, Hi, Pat." Listening....then, "You're both going to be late getting back from the football game? I see…overtime? Well, alright. Uncle Tim is already here, so we'll go ahead with dinner." After another pause, "What's that? …..Yes, I'll tell him."

She ended the call and explained to Tim that it could be late before they got home. Then, "Oh, he said you asked about the recent burglaries at several museums up and down the east coast. He apparently has some new information about them."

"Really? I hope it's some *good* news."

Tim began to set the dinner plates on the table. "Pat never takes a day off, does he? He's either working at the police station or cheering on my one-and-only favorite nephew, who just happens to be named for me." While getting silverware from the drawer, "By the way, the two of you have raised a really good kid. *And* a great quarterback!"

He started to reminisce, something Terry noticed happening more often lately. "You know, when *I* was the quarterback in high school, Pat was such a great offensive lineman, always protecting me."

Terry joined in the reflection. "Brings back some good memories of the old days, celebrating football victories when we were all in high school together. And I have to admit, being the twin sister of the team quarterback sure helped with my popularity."

"Is that why Pat started dating you?' Again, they chuckled. They always enjoyed a good laugh, which most often came spontaneously. But if it didn't, they worked hard to find a funny angle to just about anything. It was rewarding, and it contributed to their bond.

"Yeah, I miss those days, when I had more wins than losses."

"Is that why you came home?" Terry had been wanting to learn more about his reasons for returning -- more, below the surface of his previous explanation -- but the right timing hadn't shown up. Now, Tim had opened the door, and Terry walked right in.

"Yeah...like they say," (this time without the usual grin), "'When you get lost, home is a good place to get found.' And besides, I was hoping that being the twin brother of

Tiverton's computer guru, with her own
successful business, might help with *my*
popularity -- and help me find my self-
confidence again, like my old quarterback
days."

"I knew your returning home was a good
idea, at least for now. We all wondered how
you would do, being the only one of our
group to go off to the big city to become a
famous museum curator. It wasn't that we
felt left behind, but, well, the big world out
there can be a scary place. And speaking of
scary places, I know you can't afford your
own apartment right now, but sleeping in a
corner of the museum is, well, kind of
spooky, especially with only wax figures to
talk to."

Speaking slowly, Tim offered this: "Well,
it's a little complicated. I'll explain later, but
right now, I'm curious about something. Can
you access the museum's security camera?"

"Sure." Terry entered a couple of quick
commands into the computer, and they
could see the Soule-Seabury family room
and now they saw, with their own eyes, what
Jack was up to.

Chapter 20 – A plan emerges

Not aware that he was being watched by four eyes from a nearby house, Jack was gaining confidence in his effort to pull off the heist of his career. Confident enough to call his mother, the over-powering master-mind of the gang, to give her a positive update. He placed the call from a side room of the museum.

"Mom?"

"Once again, don't ever call me 'Mom' on this phone. Have you already forgotten what I told you, Mr. Muddle-head? Always use my *code* name!"

"Oh, I'm sorry Mom...err, Jill." With one word, so controlling was his mother, his confidence had plummeted.

After Jill gave a very hearable sigh, Jack continued. "Well, I called to give you an update. I know where the book is!"

"Good job. Now, grab the book and *get out of there.*"

Her demand called for a slow, hesitant response. "Well...it's not going to be that simple."

"I don't understand."

"Well...the family of wax figures is ...
reading it."

"Reading it? Oh, Son, will I *ever* be able to
trust you to actually accomplish a goal? Are
you *that* afraid of growing up?"

"Oh, Mom, *trust* me. The ghosts in this
house are *real*!"

Getting increasingly frustrated with her
adult-but-still-a-little-boy son, her voice
grew stern. "Jack, you're not a child any
more. I know its Halloween but it's time that
you let go of your fear of ghosts and be a
grownup, *for a change*."

"Like I said, it's not that simple. Look, I'm
going to develop a plan and I'll call you
back when I can get a handle on the
situation."

"But..."

Click.

***

Tim has now seen -- and heard it all, thanks
to Terry's computer security system. He sat
back in his chair and thought to himself, out

loud, "So, *that's* their game. And to think, I *trusted* him!"

Terry identified with her brother's thoughts, and emotions. "Trusting the right person at the right time is not an easy skill to find."

After a pause, true to her introvert trait, she was compelled to add a necessary observation, focusing on practical reality. "But, Tim. Those wax figures were ... *talking*!"

"Terry, I never told anyone before, but, well, those wax figures *are* real -- *sometimes*."

"Are you being *serious*?"

"*Very*...and when they *do* speak, I have learned so much about history -- *their* history, in particular. And after losing all hope, after being fired at the museum in Philadelphia, well, they helped me find my purpose again. They reminded me of how much I love history."

"Why *this* family's history?"

"Think about what they went through: their fear of a deadly pandemic, something *we* might be experiencing ourselves, 200 years later. They didn't know what to expect, just like *we* don't know what's ahead."

Though Terry was not often one to expressively speak up (in true introvert fashion), it was now time to do just that. "Well, at least we know that we'll never need the smallpox vaccine again. What a relief!"

Channeling one of his history professors, "Terry, as a museum curator, I have learned enough from history to be cautious about predicting the future! Who knows what the next few years will bring. I'm sure *they* wondered, too, with a pandemic that actually came in waves and variations, even when it seemed long over. Will that happen to *us*?'

And he had more to think about...

"I wonder...perhaps one of those smallpox waves involved losing their first child, at such a young age. Can you imagine that? I suspect George was one of the unrecognized victims of the smallpox. I'm sure they worried about that, and about their future children. Sound familiar? Who said it first? 'History's themes keep reappearing.'"

Terry was trying to follow it all, and absorb it as well. "I can't believe it, but you're beginning to make sense."

Tim slowly walked to the side of the computer table and continued reflecting out loud.

"And realizing these living figures from history are right here, in our museum, this is a chance to learn something from the past about finding hope in the midst of our own present pandemic. And there's something else. I now understand why things in the museum sometimes appear to move, or disappear."

Tim and Terry's attention returned to the security camera, as Cornelius resumed his reading and commentary.

***

"Ichabod would teach music classes, and one day…well, here is the story:"

"Among the musical disciples who assembled, one evening in each week, to receive instructions in psalmody, was Katrina Van Tassel, the daughter and only child of a substantial Dutch farmer. She was…universally famed, not merely for her beauty, but her vast expectations."

Interjecting his commentary, "And here is where the plot gets complicated:"

"From the moment Ichabod laid his eyes upon Mr. Van Tassel's vast lands with regions of delight…his only study was how to gain the affections of the peerless daughter of Van Tassel."

Commenting again, "But, there was competition for her attention. Let's see…"

***

Tim couldn't resist an observation along with his own interjection, as a historian. "I guess some things really don't change. Two hundred years later, we *still* compete over relationships."

Responding with her personal perspective, "And over wanting to influence each other's decisions. You wanted me to date *another* guy on the team."

"I remember. And I'm so glad you ignored my advice and married Pat. I should've trusted you. You made the right choice."

"Lesson learned: focus on controlling your *own* life, and not the lives of others!"

***

Cornelius continued reading about the main competitor, "the most formidable was a burly, roaring man of the name of Abraham, or, according to the Dutch abbreviation, Brom, the hero of the country round, which rang with his feats of strength and hardihood. He was broad-shouldered and double-jointed, with short curly black hair, and a bluff, but not unpleasant countenance, having a mingled air of fun and arrogance." And Cornelius added that Brom was described as known and respected "for great knowledge and skill in *horsemanship*."

Unable to hold back, Jane interrupted, "Are we getting to the part about the *headless horseman*? Will he be real, or a ghost?"

"Patience, Child. We need to read a bit more."

***

It was Tim's turn to not hold back. "Now, *I* am getting a bit scared, thinking about the possibility of *two* ghost legends colliding in the Yellow House, that of the *headless horseman* and that of *Little George*. Are either real, or just *real ghosts*"?

With a comforting tone, Terry spoke up. "Don't get too carried away, Tim."

"I know, but, what has history taught us about what we *believe*? Whether about ghosts, or illness, or ... anything? How do we know what's *real*?"

"Let's listen in again, and maybe we'll learn something."

***

Now it was Benjamin who could not hold back. Typically, he was a very strong introvert who followed a cardinal rule for that personality type: quietly listen and don't verbally repeat what has already been said. The problem with extraverts, from his view, was that they keep saying the same things over and over again, taking up verbal space without adding anything original. But if a new or alternate message needed to be stated, introverts usually speak up. Which is what Benjamin did.

Finally joining the conversation, he addressed his sister. "Jane, there is no factual evidence as to the existence of ghosts; they are alive only in your imagination. It's time to face reality."
Jane was only spurred on. "Ben, you are always ignoring the reality of hopes and dreams, which are as real as *anything* in this world. Will you finally open your mind?"

"I am *already* open-minded. If we are going to debate, critique my logic, not my beliefs."

"You are the most stubborn brother in history. Wake up!"

"And you are too wedded to your beliefs. Beliefs are important, but they are changeable. Facts are not."

Jane's limits had almost reached an end point. "Why do you always deny the reality of *anything*?"

And Benjamin's limits had also been reached, although he had a way of keeping his analytical approach to everything, even emotions. "I am not a nihilist, my sister. It's not a question of believing that *nothing* is real; it's a question of deciding *what* is real."

"But can't you see how hard it is to separate facts from beliefs. After all..."

And now it was Cornelius' turn to declare a limit -- at least to this debate. It was time for him to intervene (and it wasn't the first time). "Come, now. You are free to disagree, but you are not free to be unkind."

Allowing their father's words to sink in, Jane spoke up first. "You're right Father. Thank your reminding us -- *each* of us -- to disagree respectfully."

"And," Benjamin chimed in, "We do need to be reminded occasionally of a pledge we have taken before: to always keep our 'communication door' open, in spite of our different perspectives."

"And our different communication styles," Jane quickly added.

Cornelius added, as though it were a punctuation mark, "Good. Now let's get back to the book."

"The sights of Sleepy Hollow 'were nothing to the tales of ghosts and apparitions. The neighborhood is rich in legendary treasures of the kind. All the stories of ghosts and goblins that he had heard …now came crowding upon his recollection, approaching the very place where many of the scenes of the ghost stories had been laid.'"

Continuing, with a returning somber tone anticipating the approach of a ghostly event, referencing the foreshadowing approach of night fall, as the day "grew darker and darker, the stars seemed to sink deeper in the sky, and driving clouds occasionally hid them from his sight. He had never felt so lonely and dismal. His heart began to sink within him. On mounting a rising ground," pausing again for effect, Ichabod could see a "figure in relief against the sky, gigantic in height, and muffled in a cloak. Ichabod was horror-struck on perceiving..." that the figure...had no visible head. And continuing, "...but his horror was still more increased on observing that the head, which should have rested on his shoulders, was carried before him on the pommel of his saddle!"

And even more slowly, and almost in a whisper, "If I can but reach that bridge, thought Ichabod, 'I am safe.'"

Jane asked in a hurried pace, "Oh, my! What happened next?"

"The next morning the old horse was found without his saddle. Ichabod did not make his appearance at breakfast; dinner-hour came, but no Ichabod. The boys assembled at the schoolhouse, and strolled idly about the banks of the brook; but no schoolmaster. An inquiry was set on foot, and after diligent investigation ..."

Again in his slower, 'scary voice' for his ever-loved (and oft over-used) dramatic effect, "...they came upon his traces."

Now, even Benjamin needed to express his thoughts, but still characteristically displaying his value of focusing on observable evidence, "What did they find?"

"In one part of the road leading to the church was found the saddle trampled in the dirt; the tracks of horses' hoofs deeply dented in the road, and evidently at furious speed, were traced to the bridge, beyond which, on the bank of a broad part of the brook, where the water ran deep and black, was found..."

And now he built the reading to an even higher level of fear, in his strongest bass-level voice, "...the hat of the unfortunate

Ichabod, and close beside it...a
shattered...pumpkin."

"Oh, Father, it's starting to get scary."

Realizing that Jane may be too scared for
now, he backed away from his 'scary voice'
and returned to a normal baritone level,
with, "Then, perhaps it is time for a break.
Besides, your evening chores are still
waiting for you both, then we'll have time
enough for another reading before your
bedtimes."

He reached for his pocket watch, but
couldn't find it, as he searched through his
jacket.

"Mother, have you seen my pocket watch?"

"No, but you had it just a few minutes ago."

At that point, almost out the blue, but
actually completely in context, Jane asked,
"Father, tell me truthfully, are there *really*
ghosts around us?"

Benjamin sensed this was not the time to
speak up; he focused on listening, even more
intently than usual. He sensed that there was
a question under the question.

"Oh, Child, you don't need to be frightened, because…"

Mary quickly interrupted. "Wait a minute, Cornelius." Then, to Jane, also sensing there was more to the question, "Why do you ask that question now, Child?"

"Because, sometimes it *feels* like ghosts are real. Things happen for no reason. Sometimes good things, and sometimes bad things."

"Like what?" Mary asked.

"Like your pocket watch. How did it mysteriously disappear?"

Cornelius tried to intervene in the line of questioning, taking the question only at face value. "Well..."

"And the illness. Why do things like *that* happen?"

"You mean, the smallpox." Cornelius responded.

"And when Little George died, so young. Things like that make me sad."

Mary noted, "That was before you were even born, Child."

"I know, but I hear you and Father talking about him and about how much you miss him, and how sometimes you feel his presence." There was a silence in the room, but Jane continued, "It's not just when bad things happen. Sometimes I find lost toys in the most unexpected places. For no apparent reason! And when someone gets better after getting the illness. Things like that make me happy!"

Cornelius began to feel uncomfortable with the direction of this conversation. He often felt that way when personal, emotional topics were brought out into the open. "It's close to your bedtime, Child. We'll talk about this in the morning. And that applies to you, too, Benjamin."

They dutifully left the room, and Cornelius acknowledged to Mary, "You know the saying: 'From the mouths of babes!'" And after a pause, and in a more serious voice, "She's right about mysterious things which happen around here. Sometimes it's downright fearful!"

Mary quickly observed, "Oh, Cornelius…we all know…"

".. *And*…she makes a good point about our grieving still, over George's death. I know he was our first child…"

Reflecting, "…Born only a year after we were married," Mary added. "I felt like I had failed you, and I was so frightened for the future."

"And I felt like *I* had failed *you*, my dear. And I feared the future, as well."

Mary thought out loud, with a hint of a tear forming, "We buried so many relatives in the family cemetery during that peak of the smallpox, and then George. None of us could imagine what the future would hold."

Feeling the need to bring the conversation to a realistic focus, closer to his comfort level, "But, Mary, even with the difficulties and loses, life has still been very fulfilling, and it *has* been a *long* time, my dear. Perhaps enough time to begin to...let go."

"Oh, that's harder than anything I've ever done, which is saying a lot, after raising 11 other children! Sometimes, I think, if I let go of the *pain*, I might also be letting go of the *good* memories."

Then, after an unusually long silent moment, "Cornelius. Tell me something. Do *you* believe in ghosts?"

"Why do you ask that, now, Mary?"

"Because, if George were alive, he would be about the same age as Charles - or Tim. Don't you ever think about that?"

"To be honest, I do. It's hard *not* to. But," in his consistent approach to the difficult times in his life, "we have to face reality, dear."

In Mary's *own* consistent search for *personal* answers in difficult times, "But, what if ghosts *are* a part of reality? What if George is checking up on us, to see how we are doing since that terrible loss? Or, trying to find out how we might treat him, if he were here. Or, more importantly, perhaps George, *himself*, is in need of help, like Charles and Tim appear to be. Shouldn't we help them, since either one might be -- just *might* be -- George reaching out to us?"

Cornelius thought, and was inspired to respond, "Well, like our wise child might say, perhaps the *good* ghosts will help us - and them."

Chapter 21 – Were the "good ghosts" listening?

Tim had heard enough. "I think it's time for the 'good ghosts' to come to the rescue."

"What does that mean?" Terry asked. She was still trying to absorb it all: talking wax figures...sorting out what is *really* real...just for starters...all on Halloween!

Tim had already thought it through. "I have a plan. I'll explain later."

***

At that moment, Jane returned to the family room, looking quite relaxed, much more so than when she had left, earlier.

Her calm demeanor was quite compatible with the décor of the family room environment: a soft glow from the fireplace, casting shifting and gentle shadows and occasionally adding a comment by way of a crackle or a pop. The fireplace, essential in that era for heat, was also a major contributor to an ambience for sitting in a comfortable wing-back chair, thinking, talking...and *reading*.

"All my evening chores are finished. Can we return to the reading?"

"Yes, Child. Let's see…"

He reached for the book, which had been resting on a side table, still disguised, silently waiting to be re-discovered.

"Recall that Ichabod had disappeared and was thought to be among the dead. But here, we learn that … well, lets' continue reading."

"It is true, an old farmer, who had been down to New York on a visit several years after, and from whom this account of the ghostly adventure was received, brought home the intelligence that Ichabod Crane was still alive; that he had left the neighborhood partly through fear … and partly in mortification at having been suddenly dismissed by the heiress; that he had changed his quarters to a distant part of the country; had kept school and studied law at the same time; had been admitted to the bar; turned politician; electioneered; written for the newspapers; and finally had been made a justice of the Ten Pound Court."

"The old country wives, however, who are the best judges of these matters, maintain to this day that Ichabod was spirited away by supernatural means; and it is a favorite story often told about the neighborhood round the winter evening fire."

Jane was smiling. "So, there *is* a happy ending, after all. And Ichabod found himself, his *true* treasure. And to help everyone find their true treasure, there was a ghost -- or ghosts -- who helped!"

***

Terry now shared Jane's relief. "So there *was* a happy ending in Sleepy Hollow!"

To which Tim added, "And if we are going to learn anything from history, that requires a happy ending in Four Corners as well."

***

Cornelius was curious, and he did want to learn more from his wise daughter. "And what lessons do you think *Katrina* learned from *her* experience?"

"Well, she was probably very sad when she found out that Ichabod was really only seeking her father's wealth, which was a pretty selfish trick."

"Go on..."

"And so, she probably lost her self-confidence, at first, and then didn't trust her ability to face the future, but..."

Mary, too, wanted to learn. "Keep going, dear."

"...but in the end, she -- *and* Ichabod -- found their self-confidence and their ability to hope. So *everyone* found their true treasures."

It was for Cornelius to state the obvious. "I always knew my children were very wise."

***

Taking it all in, Tim observed, with a confident smile, "History -- and the wisdom of a child -- to the rescue, again."

***

Mary suddenly realized the late hour. And more relevant and valuable was her sense of timing in these personal moments of sharing, which came to the fore.

"Oh, my, it really *is* getting late. It's way past your bedtime, Child. Off to bed with you."

Jane was internally receptive to a good night's rest after an energy-draining day, but in true child-mode, she resisted letting that become apparent. "Oh, all right," she said, hesitatingly. And in an added effort to stall bedtime for fear she would miss out on something important, she added, "But can I say my good-night prayers here, with you?"

"Certainly, Child."

Kneeling, she began. "Thank you for Mother and Father, and for my sisters and my brothers (even Benjamin), and including Little George. And for my teachers and friends. And please watch over those who have become ill with the sickness, and for their nurses. And watch over those who are afraid at this time of the year, and for those who have been tricked for selfish reasons."

She started to stand, moving one knee for a step up. But then, she returned to her kneeling position, to add this request:

"And, finally, for Charles, the stable boy, and Tim, who both seem to have lost something. Please help them find it. Amen."

Cornelius was uncharacteristically moved, though only Mary could hear a very slight quiver in his voice. "Thank you child. Here, please put the book back on the shelf, with its disguising cover, to keep it safe."

***

Also moved were the two observers from the dining room table, in 2020, trying to absorb the moment, which took place just now...or perhaps...two centuries earlier.

Then back to reality, and the present, Terry asked, "So, what's your plan, Tim? Are we ready to have them arrested?"

"I think we have enough evidence, but I need a way to keep Jack at the museum until Pat can get there." Still thinking up a plan, "Where did I put my Halloween costume?"

He grabbed the box and started to leave.

"I'm going back to the museum. Call Pat. Tell him I need him to be a lineman again, like the old days, to protect me from a difficult situation. Have him meet me there as soon as he can…and we'll share our notes about the '*Jack and Jill Gang*.'"

Almost at the door, he turned to look back. "Oh, and keep recording this security tape."

Chapter 22 – Being found

A few minutes later, after Jane and Mary had left, Cornelius was standing by the fireplace when Jack entered the room. "Thank you Charles, for the additional firewood."

"You're welcome, Sir," Jack answered. But after stacking the wood, he returned to his *real* mission -- finding the book.

"By the way, where is the book?"

"The book? You mean the Washington Irving book?"

"Yes, that one."

"But why would a simple stable boy be interested in…"

Cornelius was interrupted by the return of Mary followed by Jane, who spoke up first, "We came in to say good night."

"Thank you, Child. Good night."

Jack now realized that it was time to get serious, and in his strongest gangster voice, he issued an order, "Don't go *anywhere* – any of you. *Where is the book?*"

Cornelius was startled. "Charles, this is not like you. Who *are* you, *really*?"

Just then, there were three, loud, ominous and slow knocks at the door.

Now Jack was startled. "Don't move!" Then realizing his power over them, "Oh, wait. I know how to make that happen!"

He quickly dialed Jill, who answered, "Jack, are you still at the museum?"

"Hold on…"

Mysteriously, this time the wax figures ***did not*** freeze.

"Wait…you're supposed to freeze! What's going on here?"

Then they all heard three more slow knocks. Jack slowly moved toward the door to even more slowly open it….only to be startled by a *headless horseman* in the doorway, holding a pumpkin!

The *headless horseman* entered the room, carrying a pumpkin which looked like his head.

Completely caught off guard, Jack dropped the cell phone -- and fainted.

Jane yelled out, "Oh, Father, it's the *headless horseman*! Is he here to hurt us?"

"No, Child. He is here to *help* us."

In rapid succession, "What? But how? Why?"

"Just wait and watch, my child, and what is meant to be clear, will be clear."

Then the *headless horseman* revealed his face. It was Tim, in his old Halloween costume.

"Father -- could Tim be a ghost?"

Jack was beginning to recover from his fall and he slowly stepped back up.

"Or, could *Charles* be a ghost?" Then, in an assertive, adult voice, "Charles, or whatever your name is, I am beginning to think that you are very, very lost."

Jack, or Charles, yelled back, channeling his mother's voice, "What do **you** know? You're just a wax dummy!"

"Don't call *me* a dummy! You're not the *only* one who can talk…"

And Mary now joined in, "or think…"

And Cornelius "…*or* figure out your game plan."

Jane, seeing this as yet another opportunity to be the "teacher-parent", dived in again, "Honestly, I think you could learn something from us, because our *present* may be your *past* -- and more -- your *future,* too!"

A confused Jack replied, "What do you mean?"

It was now Tim's turn. "Think about it, Jack. All that *they* have been through, and all that *we* are going through?"

Yet another ominous knock came from the door, not once, but three times, as if sending a code. It made everyone, wax and human, temporarily freeze. Until Tim slowly moved toward the door.

Before he could get to the door, the wax figures froze in place.

When Tim finally reached the door, he opened slowly, arm extended, as if preparing to invite the grand entrance of George Washington himself.

It was, however, Pat, Terry's husband, now in the role as the local Police Chief. He looked at Tim and offered a slight bow, to play out his grand welcome. He also had a newspaper article in his hand, which he waved as though it were a flag in a parade.

Relieved to see a friend, and the police, "Pat! I'm so glad you're here. And your timing is perfect."

"Good evening, Tim. I got the message from Terry. You sent for me?"

"Yes, I did." And then he made his special announcement, "May I introduce half of the *Jack and Jill Gang*!"

Tim picked up the cell phone and handed it to Pat.

"Funny you should mention that gang," Pat responded. "Here's the information I just found out about them. It's from a Philadelphia newspaper."

Reading the news story print-out, "Another *Jack and Jill Heist*! A local museum was robbed last night by a couple who left this note at the counter: 'We thank you for your historical treasure. Signed: Jack and Jill.'

They took a priceless, signed, first edition book and several very valuable pocket watches, one of which was 200 years old. This was their second heist at the same museum."

"Their *second* heist?" Tim repeated. It was an 'aha' moment, as he is put the pieces of the puzzle together. "At my old museum!"

"Where you were fired because of mysteriously missing items -- which they thought YOU stole."

"Probably the ones Jack and Jill stole in their *first* heist. It's all beginning to add up."

Pat began to connect the dots. "It appears that Jill is the 'wizard behind the curtain' in the outfit. Their MO is to blend in with the tourists for the last tour of a museum's season, hide as the curator leaves, then take out a few select, and very valuable items. And the theft would not be discovered until the next season's opening."

Tim continued to think it through, out loud. "And when I caught him, here, he had to change his MO."

Pat, clarifying his role as the chief investigator, "We'll check the security tapes to see if he took anything."

"Now, wait a minute." As if to begin his defense, Jack jumped into the conversation. "I have witnesses that I didn't actually take any book from here."

Pat had to ask. "*Witnesses*?"

Jack gained some confidence and assertively explained. "Yes, the Soule-Seabury Family, *here*."

In disbelief, Pat continued his 'interrogation'. "These wax figures? *They* are going to testify on your behalf?"

"Yeah! I'll show you. Give me the cell phone."

Disbelieving, but faithful to his duty to allow Jack to explain before being arrested, Pat handed him the phone and Jack spoke into it, to Jill, who was still there, since the phone call had never ended.

"Jill? Are you still there? It's me. I'm going to end our call so the wax figures will come to life, again."

"Oh, son. You really *are* a disappointment!"

He ended the call, but, now the wax figures do **_not_** return to life.

Jack was in shock. "I don't get it..."

Pat finally knew what he needed to do. "I don't know what you're talking about, but you'd better come with me..."

Taking the cell phone, he began to place handcuffs on his prisoner, adding "And it looks like we know how to reach Jill."

Still trying to figure out what was happening, Jack kept talking. "But - but - they come to life when I get off the phone..."

Starting to walk him toward the door, "Sure, sure, son. Come along. Don't make it any harder on yourself."

Jack continued, "Why aren't they alive again?"

And then...

He suddenly assessed his situation, and as suddenly, he seemed to find the glimmer of an actual conscience.

"Wait -- wait. I think this family is trying to teach me something," and he stopped to take in a very deep breath.

"OK...I'll give you a complete confession. And... I need to return *this*."

He reached into his jacket to return the pocket watch.

"And I agree to return everything I took from the Philadelphia Museum...to you, Tim ...so your reputation will be restored."

"And you'll be pleased to know that more than *that* will be restored," explained Pat. "There's a reward for solving the Philadelphia caper. And I guess that will go to *you*, Tim."

"And most of that will go to our museum, to get us back on our feet. But Jack, why the change of heart?"

"Well, I've got nothing to lose, but maybe something to gain. I can't really explain it. I just now felt a, a light wind, like a breath of fresh air, and for some mysterious reason, I suddenly realized that I wasn't really trusting myself." Thinking differently than he ever had, allowing a new reality to sink in, "Even Jill…I mean Mom…she didn't trust in me. I have actually learned something here, including, how important trust *is*…trusting ourselves, trusting others, and how important it is that others trust *us*."

"Trust is hard to find, but easy to lose." observed Tim.

"And there's something else I found," Jack admitted. "I actually *do* like history. I figure it's never too late to turn a new page in my *personal* history book."

Tim thought for a moment, and decided to say out loud what he was feeling, deep within his heart. "If you're serious, I'll testify on your behalf that you never hurt anyone, and that you appear to have, well, *found yourself*."

Jack reflected on the entire event here inside the *Yellow House*. "It's pretty amazing that a group of people from the past can help someone in the present to, *get found*."

"Yes it is. Let's hope our future museum patrons will learn that, too."

Pat escorted Jack through the door, leaving behind Tim, and the frozen wax figures.

Who, mysteriously...

came back to life again.

Predictably, Tim was not surprised. "Ah, I guess I owe you a word of thanks."

"Well, as your generation would say, 'No problem, bro.'" Adding, "And... I have to admit, we have enjoyed some of the comedy of this adventure. As Washington Irving, himself, added at the end of his story: 'There is no situation in life [without] its advantages and pleasures -- provided we will but take a joke as we find it.'"

They all chuckled.

"But I must confess, I wondered how long it would take for you to figure it all out."

Jane, who had been carefully observing the last few minutes, spoke up to ask, "Father, speaking of 'figuring it all out', what did you mean when you said, 'what is *meant* to be clear, will be clear'"?

"First, Child, you wouldn't really want *every* mystery to be solved; if that were the case, life would be pretty boring. Mysteries are... the soul of curiosity, of learning, and of hope. Who would ever want to lose those gifts? And, second, when you get older, you'll learn that some mysteries are simply not meant to be solved. Some, we don't really *want* to know, and some, we don't *need* to know."

"I don't understand."

Mary then took her turn to offer advice. "You will, Child. One day, you will."

Then Tim needed to ask about a mystery of his own. "Speaking of mysteries, why didn't you come to life when Jack ended the call to Jill, when Pat was here?"

For Cornelius, the answer was obvious. "Because Pat was not ready to learn about us. And you still have more to learn about how we figures from the past work, my son."

"And I'll bet the security tapes will no longer reveal anything about your coming to life?"

"Right, you are, my son. They will be among the several mysterious disappearances surrounding this whole encounter."

Recognizing his novice status as a ghost finder, as well as a *self*-finder, "I guess I do have more to learn, especially since I now feel like a member of the family... *your* family, here at the museum."

"You can begin to think of yourself as George's older brother," Mary said, softy.

To which Jane had an important query, "Does that mean you will come back to bring us the book, so we can re-read 'The Legend of Sleepy Hollow?'"

"Since we won't have to sell the book to save the museum, we'll leave it in the bookcase for your father to read at night, when the crowds have gone home. And we will be sure to disguise it each night!"

"Oh, thank you, Tim."

And Mary offered one more, poignant comment for Tim. "And speaking of George, I want to thank *you*, too."

"What do you mean?"

"After tonight, I think it may be time to begin to let go of that pain."

"Knowing what to hold on to and what to let go of, can be a difficult process. Just don't ever let go of the lessons, or the blessings of the past -- or the *hope*. *Especially* the hope. I know *that* from experience. And I think I have found that hope, again. And I'm sure you will, too, Mary."

Jane smiled...no grinned, from waxy ear to waxy ear. "We'll all help each other, from now on. And that's a promise."

The wax figures moved to their pre-tour positions where they resumed their frozen status. And Tim started to the door.

But just has he placed his hand on the door knob, ready to open the door, Jane came back to life.

"Oh, Tim, you win this year's contest for the scariest costume!"

And Tim smiled, as he walked through the doorway, toward his newfound life.

Chapter 23 – At the cemetery

Three Weeks later...

The fog drifted in to hover over both old and new tombstones in the Soule-Seabury family cemetery.

It was expectedly quiet; not even the evening birds were conversing.

Until...

Tim arrived. Though he was not talking, the birds could probably have heard his breathing.

He had come for a moment of reflection, and to bring a single flower, for Little George's grave. He knew where the tombstone was, for he had been here before, but tonight was different.

"Well, George, I'm not sure where to begin. First, as a student of history, I want you to know that I've recently learned a lot about your family, and, in particular, I learned that they loved – I mean *love* -- you very much. You may be a ghost to some, but as far as I'm concerned, you are very much alive, to all of us at the museum and to your family."

As he stood in silence before the simple and worn grave marker, a figure took form from the mist.

It was Cornelius, also bringing a flower.

Tim was surprised. "Cornelius? What brings *you* here?"

"I expected you to be here, my son, to find some closure to our little adventure."

Sensing an open door, he entered, asking, "Speaking of closure, can I ask you something?"

"I also expected you to ask some questions, beyond these recent events. Perhaps about our future, mine *and* yours?"

"Well, yes...but how did you know that?" Then as quickly as he had said that, "Oh, never mind, I keep forgetting that you are from another world."

"In my world, reality is not so much *another* world as another *encounter* with the same world. Go ahead with your questions, Son."

Tim had so many questions, but after a moment to internally edit his list, he asked, "If we *are* at the beginning of a new pandemic in our own time, what can we learn from *your* generation's pandemic? An illness is one thing to survive, but the debates and proposals these days are another, as they have become so divisive. How will we survive *that*?"

"Even though I can see *our* future in this present moment, no one can see the *yet-to-be-lived* future. But I can offer some observations."

His pace and presentation was a bit more measured now, pondering the significant question at hand.

"In our time," he began, "the responses to the smallpox were also very controversial, whether it was President Washington's inoculation mandate for the military, or even Benjamin Franklin's shifting his own position on whether to oppose or support inoculations. Living with those disagreements were indeed very difficult for us. And I can predict that you, too, will face similar controversies; that is one thing I have learned from history: its themes do seem to resurface. And another history lesson has taught me that as time progresses, society becomes more and more complicated. And with increased complexity comes increased conflict."

In a thankful and hopeful manner, Tim interjected, "As a historian, I would value *any* advice from your time."

Cornelius paused to reflect a moment before continuing, a common sign of wisdom.

"As a practical businessman, I have learned the value of weighing costs with benefits. Not just in business, but in *everything*. For your generation, as in ours, the answers are found in weighing the balance of *independence* -- what we fought for in our own time, with *obligations* -- why we chose a democracy which united our 13 states, with shared responsibilities."

Tim needed to hear more. "But how do we accomplish that today, given our intense divisions?"

"The answer is found in the *process* of increasing the quality of understanding each other's beliefs and actions."

Again, another pause, to decide on what to focus on, in the direction of some very practical advice.

"In my world of business transactions, I most often weighed things by a scale of pennies and ounces, but in the human world, the best scale is one which weighs truth with consequences."

To which Tim asked the obvious question, "And how can that actually be measured?"

"By a special approach to communication, one which involves listening with a *third* ear."

"A third ear?"

"By adding your *heart* to your ears. Over time, we ghosts have learned that skill. And, for your closure, I offer it as a parting gift."

Another pause before his conclusion.

"Please, never stop listening to each other."

After a silent pause, for reflection, Tim thought out loud, "I wonder how we will ever be able to focus on that."

"Perhaps the 'good ghosts' will help..." came the reply.

Cornelius bent to place his flower on the grave, and slowly backed out of site.

Never seeing Cornelius, Terry entered the cemetery. She had not been here before, but she saw Tim as she entered the cemetery through the small wrought iron gate.

She was also bringing a flower.

"Oh, Tim. It looks like we're on the same page, thinking about the same things. And accidentally choosing the same single flowers."

Tim wondered if it was truly accidental, or....

Then another figure approached. It was Jack, also with a flower, also of the same kind.

He saw both Tim and Terry, but did not speak. He paused by the tombstone to look down.

Tim couldn't resist. "Why are *you* here? To rob the grave?"

"I deserve that, but actually, I am here to, well, apologize. Not to *you* -- I've already done that. But to George."

Then, to the tombstone, "I'm sorry I took advantage of you, George, for my own personal gain."

Then they each placed a flower on the grave, at the base of the marker, almost as if it had been choreographed, with a moment of recognition that they were united in this action.

After placing the flowers, Jack took a moment to visually count (by pointing and mouthing) the number of flowers: 4.

Then he did the same to count the people present: 3.

He looked confused. Tim and Terry both hunched their shoulders to non-verbally say, "It's a mystery."

After another pause, he looked at Tim and Terry to ask, "By the way, why are *you* here?"

Tim answered first. "After our experience here, I realize even more that history is both real and much more than a window into the *past*, but also a window into the *present.*"

Terry nodded in agreement, and added, "I guess all three of us really *are* on the same page. Not here in a cemetery to focus on the dead, but to focus on the *living*, especially those from history who had a rough life with lots of similarities to today, as they found a way to live through it. They *survived*. And that teaches us that *we* will survive; we don't have to live in fear of the future."

"Or, even in fear of ghosts," added Tim.

Jack expressed his caution, "Now, let's not get *too* sentimental."

"Let's also not get too *cynical*. After all, whoever said it first, 'Those who ignore history will never find out anything from it.' We need to remember that we can have hope only *if* we find those lessons from our past."

Then, addressed to George's grave, "Thank you, George, for reminding us of that."

He made a quarter-turn, to walk away, but quickly turned back to squarely face the marker, to add, "Oh, and, George, have no fear. Your family is fine. You may rest in peace."

Then, in unison without any planning, Tim and Terry turned and started walking back to the gate. But Jack stopped them.

"One more question for the two of you: In your mind, who – or what – haunts this house?"

Tim wasn't sure what to say. "Well, I just..." motioning toward where Cornelius had stood, but they didn't know that.

"I mean...we are here..." gesturing toward the tombstone.

"But...But..."

And then, after a sigh of resignation to the fact that it can't be easily explained, "I guess that's still an unsolved mystery, my friend."

They looked at the grave, then at each other, then again at the grave...and silently walked into the mist.